Pants

to P.C. – G.A.
for Lucy – N.S.

PANTS
A PICTURE CORGI BOOK 978 0 552 55572 2
First published in Great Britain by David Fickling Books,
a division of Random House Children's Books
A Random House Company

David Fickling edition published 2002
Picture Corgi edition published 2003
This edition published 2006

5 7 9 10 8 6 4

Text copyright © Giles Andreae, 2002
Illustrations copyright © Nick Sharratt, 2002

The right of Giles Andreae and Nick Sharratt to be identified as the author
and illustrator of this work has been asserted in accordance
with the Copyright, Designs and Patents Act 1988.

Picture Corgi Books are published by Random House Children's Books,
61–63 Uxbridge Road, London W5 5SA

www.**rbooks**.co.uk
www.**kids**at**randomhouse**.co.uk

Addresses for companies within The Random House Group Limited can be found at:
www.randomhouse.co.uk/offices.htm

THE RANDOM HOUSE GROUP Limited Reg. No. 954009

A CIP catalogue record for this book is available from the British Library.

Printed in China

Pants

Giles Andreae
Nick Sharratt

BOOKSTART
PLUS

Picture Corgi

Small pants, big pants

Giant frilly pig pants

New pants, blue pants, one, two, three

Swinging on the door pants

How many more pants can you see?

Loose pants, tight pants

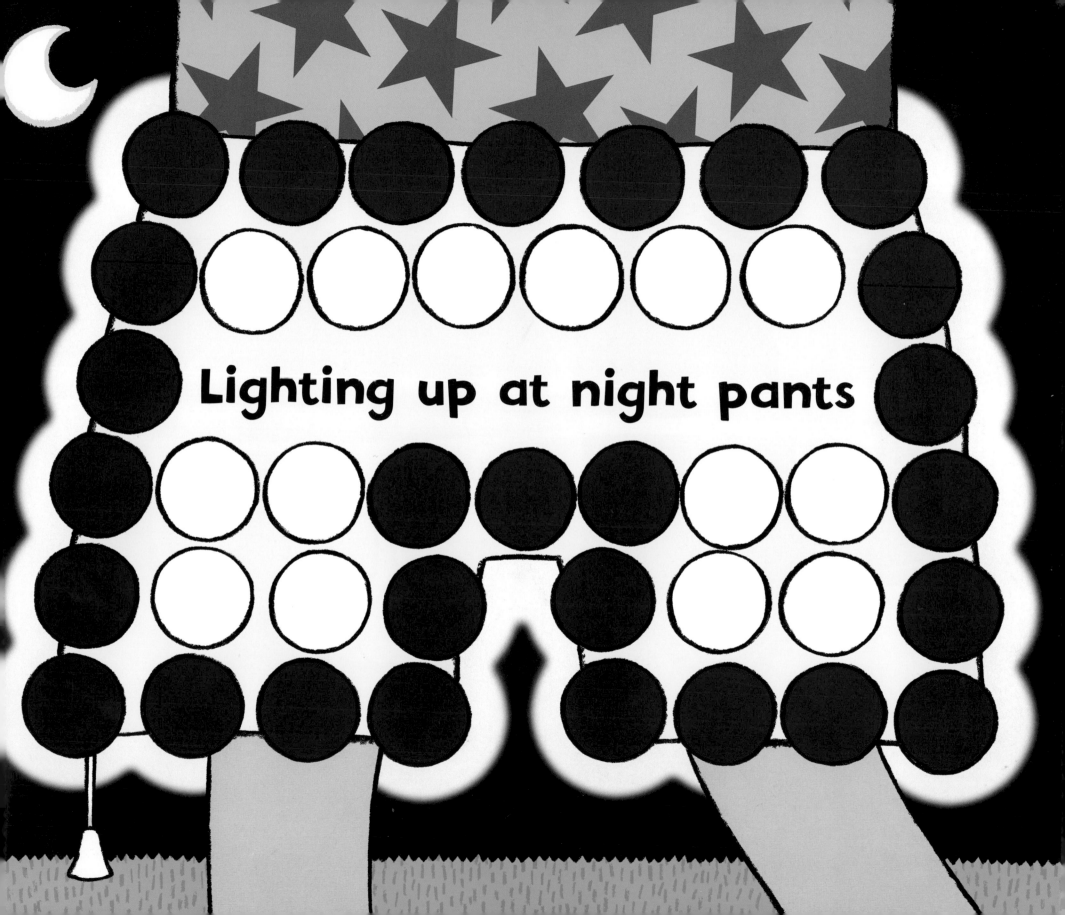

Lighting up at night pants

no pants at all!

Pants on your head
when you've gone crazy!

Funny pants,
money pants

Wear them when it's sunny pants

Have you seen these bunny pants?

Wear them when
You're happy pants

Little baby
nappy pants

Special pants for driving in the car!

Fairy pants, hairy pants

What a lot of lovely

pants there are!

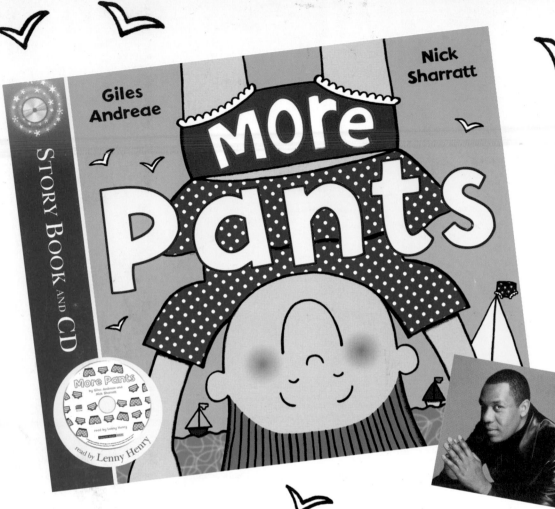